MISTS
ON
THE
RIVER

MISTS ON THE RIVER

Folktales from Siberia

by Yeremei Aipin

Gennady Raishev
Illustrator

Marina Aipin
Russian-English Translator

Claude Clayton Smith
American Editor / Translator

Shanti Arts Publishing
Brunswick, Maine

MISTS ON THE RIVER
Folktales from Siberia

Published by Shanti Arts Publishing
Shanti Arts LLC
193 Hillside Road
Brunswick, Maine 04011
shantiarts.com

This book was published as *Little Cranberry & Grassy
Braid* in Khanty-Mansiysk in 2016, adapted from the
series *Old Stories of the Surgut Ostyaks*, by Yeremei Aipin.

Interior and cover design by Shanti Arts Designs
All illustrations by Gennady Raishev

Printed in the United States of America

ISBN: 978-1-951651-40-4 (softcover)

Library of Congress Control Number: 2020941206

In memory of
Alexander Vashchenko
(1947–2013)

*[Even a] child instinctively comprehends
that although these stories are unreal,
they are not untrue.*

— Bruno Bettelheim

 Contents

❄ Foreword ❄

Far, far away—along the Ob River near the Arctic Circle in Russia—live the native people of Siberia, the clans of the Khanty and Mansi. In the old days they were called the Ostyaks and Voguls. They hunted, fished, herded reindeer, and picked delicious berries. In the evening they would gather around the wisest story-teller to hear him sing songs, tell fairy tales, and delight them with riddles about the Earth, the Sun, and Moon, as well as the animals, the birds, and fish. My grandparents listened to this wise man in their youth, and everything they learned they passed on to my parents, who passed it on to my sisters and me, in turn. In this way, from the distant past, the fairy tale heroes of our nation have come down to us: Plump Rosy Cranberry and Wispy Braided Grass; Birdie-Birdie; the Cuckoo; the Sandpiper; Paki the Bear; Lanny the Fisherman; Ptichek and his Sister; and others. I hope you will get to know these folk heroes and count them among your own.

✷ Plump Rosy Cranberry ✷ and Wispy Braided Grass

Once upon a time Plump Rosy Cranberry shared a home with Wispy Braided Grass. Every morning Rosy Cranberry would get up first, light the birch-bark kindling in the fireplace, and do the cooking when the firewood was blazing. Braided Grass did the other household chores. And that's how they lived.

One morning, however, Rosy Cranberry said, "I always get up first. Why don't *you* get up first and light the kindling?"

"What about my wisps?" said Braided Grass. "They could catch on fire."

"What are the chances of that?" Rosy Cranberry said.

"Fine," Braided Grass agreed. "I'll light the kindling tomorrow."

The next morning Braided Grass got up first, dressed, and lit the slivers of birch bark. And soon the firewood was blazing. But a gust of wind caught the fire and shot a spark to the

wisps of Braided Grass, who suddenly burst into flame. Sitting on the bed, Rosy Cranberry laughed and laughed—until Rosy Cranberry burst apart.

And that was the end of Plump Rosy Cranberry and Wispy Braided Grass!

Birdie-Birdie's Bow and Arrows

"**B**irdie-Birdie, where are your bow and arrows?"
"On the stump."
"Where's the stump?"
"A fire burned it."
"Where's the fire?"
"The rain put it out."
"Where's the rain?"
"The Sun took it."
"Where's the Sun?"
"A cloud hid it."
"Where's the cloud?"
"The wind took it."
"Where's the wind?"
"It blew away."

✼ The Cuckoo ✼

Once upon a time a hunter's family lived in a small dwelling in the forest. One day, when Father went hunting, Mother sat on their bed, cutting out patterns on her sewing board and working her needle and thread with her thimble to sew them. She was making warm clothes for the family for the coming winter. Her children, a boy and a girl, were playing games. When Mother became thirsty, she asked her children: "Please bring me some water!"

"Soon," said her son.

"Soon," said her daughter, who was caught up in their game.

Well, Mother was in a hurry to finish her sewing because winter was coming. She had no time to fetch water, so she said, "Please fetch me some water, my son!"

"Soon," the son replied.

Then she said to her daughter, "I'm so thirsty! Please fetch me some water!"

But her daughter answered like her son, "Soon."

So Mother kept sewing and the children kept playing, instead of bringing her water. Soon Mother's thirst began to torment her. So she asked yet again, "Son, please bring me water! My mouth is dry!"

"Soon," said her son.

Mother asked her daughter again, but she answered as before. Engrossed in their games, the children had lost track of time, and so Mother kept sewing.

Before long, Mother couldn't speak. Her mouth was completely dry. She became angry, dropping her thimble and sewing board, and the sewing board split in two. As she picked up the pieces, they turned into wings. Then she tossed her thimble over her shoulder and it became a tail. Flapping her wings, she became a cuckoo bird and flew from the dwelling into a nearby tree. Her mouth was so dry she could only make one sound: "Cuck-oooo! Cuck-oooo!" Seeing this, the children ran out with a pot of water.

"Here you are, Mother!" said the son. "Drink this water!"

"Take the water, Mother!" said the daughter. "Please!"

"Don't fly away like a cuckoo!" said the son.

"Here's your water!" said the daughter. "Please come back!"

But it was too late. The Mother-Cuckoo wasn't listening. She flew from tree to tree, crying "Cuck-oooo! Cuck-oooo!"

Her children ran after her, calling and calling.

"Mommy, have some water! Come home!"

"Here's your water! Come back!"

"Come back to us!"

"Come back!"

The children ran for a long time, calling and calling. They ran so far that their bare feet became scratched and bloody, and to this day the shores of the rivers in the forest are red from their blood. Bushes with red bark—known as Pussy Willows—grow near these rivers.

And in the spring, when the cuckoo returns to the forest, all the women at home hear her cry: "Cuck-oooo! Cuck-oooo!" Then these women warn their children sternly: "Never make fun of a cuckoo! It's really an unhappy Mother whose children didn't listen to her."

The Sandpiper

"Sandpiper, Sandpiper, what is your nose?"

"My nose is an icepick."

"Sandpiper, Sandpiper, what are your eyes?"

"My eyes are two pots of water."

"Sandpiper, Sandpiper, what are your feet?"

"My feet are two forks for the fire."

"Sandpiper, Sandpiper, what is your neck?"

"My neck is a pole for the clothesline."

"Sandpiper, Sandpiper, what is your back?"

"My back is a bridge for the stream."

"Sandpiper, Sandpiper, what is your belly button?"

"My belly button is a little bag for lint."

"Sandpiper, Sandpiper, what are your ribs?"

"My ribs are rafters for the roof."

"Sandpiper, Sandpiper, what are your wings?"

"But the Sandpiper just whistled, spread its wings, and flew away."

❧ Paki the Bear ❧

Once upon a time, in the very old days, a hunter found an orphaned bear cub in the forest. Taking him home, he fed him, gave him water, and named him Paki. And so the bear cub began his new life.

The hunter's family fed Paki the same food and drink that they ate and drank themselves, sharing the last few crumbs and the very last drops equally. They didn't deprive Paki of anything as he grew up among them. When he became old enough, the hunter tied a piece of bark with a string to Paki's left forepaw and led him into the forest. After kissing and hugging him, the hunter bid him farewell. "This isn't the end, Paki," he said, "because you will live here in the forest where you were born." And so the hunter parted from the bear cub he had raised.

Well, the years passed, and one day the hunter went off on a long hunting trip into a thick forest far away. There he set up his camp and built a small hut. One day, returning from hunting, he hung his bow and quiver of arrows on a tree branch, cooked his food over a fire, and sat down to eat. Suddenly he heard a twig snap and saw a bear coming toward him. Jumping up quickly, he grabbed his bow and arrows, drew his bowstring, and aimed at the bear.

But what was this? The bear lay down on the ground, raised his left forepaw, and growled as if he wanted to say something. Surprised, the hunter lowered his bow. Then the bear got up and moved toward him. So the hunter drew his bow again, and again the bear lay down and raised his paw. What is he doing? the hunter wondered, lowering his bow once more. Again the bear got up and came toward him, and in this way he moved closer and closer to the fire. Then the hunter saw the piece of bark tied to his paw and understood.

"Well," he said happily, "it's Paki, my bear-brother!" As he set aside his bow and arrows, the bear came right to up to him, and the hunter kissed and hugged him joyfully. Then he tussled with him, murmuring many warm words, and brushing every hair of his fur. Finally, he shared the food and drink from his pot.

After dinner Paki raised his paw, and the hunter realized what had happened. The bear had grown so large that the string on the bark was hurting him. Loosening the knot, he adjusted the bark and said to Paki, "Your paw is fine, now. Go and live in peace in your forest."

But to his surprise, the bear showed no signs of leaving. The day grew dark, and when the hunter lay down to sleep, Paki lay down nearby.

During the night the hunter woke to a sudden terrible roar. Jumping up, he saw a huge beast, similar to a bear, rushing into camp. It came crashing through the trees and roaring frightfully. This beast was much bigger than Paki, and the hunter had no time to get to his bow and arrows. But Paki dashed out to grapple with the strange monster, and they rolled in the dark in a furious tangle. The bear and the beast ripped each other with their claws and fangs and beat each other with their thick paws. Grabbing his bow, the hunter was afraid to loose an arrow for fear he would hit Paki. He couldn't tell Paki from the beast in the mass of rolling fur. So he cried out, "Say something, Paki! Say something!"

Paki answered with a groan so the hunter knew where to shoot, and he shot arrow after arrow at the beast.

Whenever the beast rolled on top of him, Paki called out from beneath, and the hunter shot into the top of the massive tangle. And in this way they defeated the strange beast. Paki had saved the hunter from certain death.

After the exhausting struggle, the hunter tended Paki's wounds, fed him, gave him something to drink, and hugged him tightly. In the morning, after casting an eye around the camp, Paki headed into the forest in the direction from which he had come. And that was the last time the hunter ever saw him.

The old people often remember this story of the hunter and his bear-brother, Paki, and happily tell it to their children. What's more, unlike other tales that are often told, they insist that this one is true.

🌱 Lanny the Fisherman 🌱

Lanny the Mouse was a fisherman. He took his oars, sat in his little boat, and floated downstream. As he rowed with the current he sang this little song: "Little oars, pull my boat — pull, pull, pull. I shall have fish soon enough!"

Soon, on the left bank of the river, a village appeared, and the village children, seeing Lanny, called out, inviting him to join them.

"Land on this bank, Lanny!"

"We'll give you tea!"

"We'll feed you the head of a big fish!"

But Lanny sat in his boat as if he hadn't heard them. Keeping his eyes straight ahead, he rowed for the middle of the river. "Well," he said. "I have the head of a big fish at home." So he continued on his way, singing: "Little oars, pull my boat — pull, pull, pull. I shall have fish soon enough."

Before long a village appeared on the right bank of the river. Seeing Lanny, the children there called out:

"Land on this bank, Lanny!"

"We'll give you tea!"

"We'll feed you the tail of a big fish!"

But Lanny sat in his boat as if he hadn't heard them, keeping his eyes straight ahead. "Well," he said to himself, "I have the tail of a big fish at home."

And so he floated farther downstream, singing his song: "Little oars, pull my boat — pull, pull, pull. I will have fish soon enough."

Then a third village appeared on the left bank. It was very large, and many people stood on the shore. And the children, seeing Lanny, immediately called out:

"Land here, quickly!"

"We'll serve you tea, Lanny!"

"We'll serve you fish porridge!"

"Land here!"

Hearing only the words *fish porridge*, Lanny rowed hard for shore. That delicious porridge was his favorite treat, and he couldn't pass it up.

The moment his boat reached shore, Lanny threw down his oars and leaped to the bank. Then the children surrounded him and led him off to one of the homes.

There they sat Lanny at a table, gave him a big spoon, and brought him a pot of porridge. Lanny ate with such passion that the spoon was a blurr in his hand! He ate heartily, stopping only to praise the tasty porridge, as he devoured one pot after another. Before long, Lanny was so full that he couldn't sit up. He leaned his elbow on a nearby plank bed, but refused to let go of his spoon.

Then two children ran in, yelling:

"Lanny, the naughty boy of our village has pushed your boat out into the river! The current has taken it away!"

Lanny leaped up and ran out with his spoon, and all the noisy children ran after him. When he was almost to the river, Lanny stumbled and fell and his stomach split wide open. He rolled on the ground, in great danger of dying.

"How can we help him?" the children clamored. "What can we do?"

They ran to a neighboring village to fetch a girl who was known for her sewing.

This girl returned with them with her needles and thread and straight away stitched up Lanny's stomach. In this way she saved Lanny's life.

The children were so happy.

"Your boat has been found," one of them said. "It was caught in a tree branch along the shore."

And so, having had his fill of fish, Lanny sat in his narrow boat and rowed away.

❧ Ptichek and His Sister ❧

Once upon a time there lived a little bird named Ptichek who had a younger sister called Chi-Chi. One winter morning Ptichek flew off to hunt for food. He flew and he flew, which made him very hungry. Then he saw a house in the forest and landed there. No one was home, so Ptichek flew right in, looking for food. Behind the chimney he found a pot of melted fat. But no sooner did he sit down to eat than a large ugly Ogre staggered into the house. Grabbing Ptichek, the Ogre spoke in a rasping, gleeful voice: "Aha! I've got you! You are the hundredth naughty rascal I've caught! Now I'll kindle a fire in the fireplace and roast you on a spit! What a tiny morsel of food has come to visit! Oh-ho-ho!"

Then Ptichek replied:

"Let me go! Even if you eat me, you won't be full! So let me go!"

The Ogre held Ptichek to his ear and said, "I can't hear you. What are you chirping about?"

Ptichek repeated what he had said: "I'm so

small, you won't be full after you eat me! So let me go!"

The Ogre began to think, which is very difficult for Ogres. What Ptichek had said seemed reasonable: Ptichek was small, barely a mouthful. So the Ogre thought a bit more and then asked: "What greater piece of food can you give me in exchange?"

"I'll give you my little sister, Chi-Chi," Ptichek said.

The Ogre thought some more and said, "If you do, I'll marry her. And I'll let you go after the marriage. So be it!"

"I'll give her to you," Ptichek chirped. "I will!"

So they set off for Ptichek's sister. But as they left, the Ogre asked: "How can I keep up with you? You'll fly through the air!"

"I'll touch the snow with my wingtip," Ptichek said. "Just follow my tracks at your leisure, and you will come to our house."

"Very well," agreed the Ogre. "Let's do as you say."

So Ptichek flew on home, touching the snow with the tip of his wing, and the Ogre tramped after him, following the tracks in the new-fallen snow.

When Ptichek reached home he said to his sister, "The Ogre is coming! Kindle a fire in the fireplace, and stick the point of the icepick in there. Then boil some water in the large kettle." As Chi-Chi did this, Ptichek began to dig an enormous pit just inside the front door.

Many weeks later the ground began to shake. Then the house itself shook. The Ogre was approaching the village. When he arrived at Ptichek's house, however, he couldn't fit through the door, whether he tried to enter head first or sideways.

"Come in backwards," Ptichek suggested.

"Yes," his sister cried. "Come in backwards!"

The Ogre obeyed. Bending over, he backed through the door and immediately fell into the pit. Then Ptichek took the heated icepick from the fireplace and stabbed the Ogre, and his sister poured boiling water on him. And so the forest Ogre breathed his last breath and died.

Ptichek and his sister dragged the Ogre outside, started a huge bonfire, and pushed the

Ogre into it. But when they went back inside, a great wind came up and swirled the ashes from the fire. Then up from the ground came the muffled voice of the Ogre: "Let every cinder of my ashes become a mosquito, and let the mosquitoes suck human blood!"

Hearing this, Ptichek rushed back outside and tried to cover the remains of the fire with birch bark, but there wasn't time. The wind swirled harder, blowing the ashes all over the world, and since that very day mosquitoes appeared every summer. On the other hand, all the Ogres were gone.

"Well," Ptichek told Chi-Chi, "at least mosquitoes are not as big as blood-thirsty Ogres. We'll learn to get along somehow!"

So he filled up the pit inside the house, where he lived happily and safely with his sister, while the people of the world learned to live with mosquitoes.

The Wife and the Sandpiper

Once upon a time there lived a wife and her husband. One day when the husband went off hunting, he checked his snares and found that he'd caught a sandpiper. So he brought it home to his wife and said, "Here, you can cook this."

His wife kindled a fire in the fireplace, put the sandpiper in a kettle of water, and hung the kettle above the fire. When the sandpiper was cooked, its fat began to rise, so the wife ladled out some broth with the fat into a bowl. Then she blew the fat from the bowl to skim it away.

Well, the wife was surprised — the more she blew on the bowl, the more the fat kept rising to the top, without end. So she said to her husband: "What a fat sandpiper you caught! I've got a bowlful of fat!"

"Well," her husband said, "get another bowl and keep blowing the fat away."

So the wife got another bowl, but soon that bowl was full, too. "What should I do?" she asked her husband.

"Get a third bowl," he said. "Keep blowing the fat from the broth."

But the fat kept rising and rising. When the third bowl was full, the wife took a fourth. Then she cried: "All my bowls are full of fat. I haven't any left!"

Her husband answered from a bench by the fireplace: "Take an empty cooking pot. Blow, blow off the fat!"

Soon all the cooking pots were full of fat. So the wife filled all her cups. Then she cried to her husband: "I've no more empty dishes. Where should I blow all this fat?"

"Blow it onto the floor," the husband said. "Keep blowing!"

So the wife blew the fat to the floor. Then she cried, "It's up to my ankles!"

"Keep blowing," her husband said.

"Now it's up to my waist!"

"Keep blowing."

"Now it's up to my chest!"

"Keep blowing."

"Now my shoulders!"

"Keep blowing."

"Now my chin!"

"Keep blowing."

"Now the fat's in my mouth!"

"Keep . . . blowing! . . . Keep . . . blow—"

Then—glug! glug!—the wife choked on the fat.

And then—glug! glug!—the husband choked on the fat.

Then the house filled up to the rafters with the fat of the sandpiper, and the wife and her husband drowned within it.

Yeremei Aipin

❧ About the Author ❧

Yeremei Aipin, the son of a hunter and fisherman, was born in the village of Varyogan in West Siberia in 1948. Ethnically, he is of the Khanty people. As a young man he worked in the Siberian oil fields, then as a carpenter, before turning to creative writing at the Literary University in Moscow. Subsequently, he spent a decade at the Center for the Native Arts in Khanty-Mansiisk, where he later established the Native Heritage Park, a museum and sacred-place memorial known as Torurn Maa.

Much of Aipin's career has been devoted to politics, working on behalf of the Khanty people as a member of the Duma, the parliament of the Russian State. He is the editor of a monthly newspaper, *The Word of the Peoples of the North*. His writing has been translated into German, Finnish, Hungarian, English, and several languages spoken by Muslims around the world.

Gennady Raishev

❄ About the Illustrator ❄

Gennady Raishev is the son of a Khanty hunter. In 1954 he began his studies at Hertzen University in St. Petersburg (then Leningrad), specializing in Russian literature. After his second year, he began classes at the evening art school as well, ultimately graduating with a dual degree. It was not until the 1990s that his gift as an artist received national recognition with many solo shows. His permanent studio in Khanty-Mansiisk now serves as a memorial museum and is open to the public. Raishev's style is unique, expressive, and readily recognizable, as his illustrations of Aipin's tales demonstrate. He is influenced by Khanty legends and mythology. Raishev employs black-and-white techniques mainly in printmaking, but works in oil and watercolor as well. "Art must be mysterious," Raishev says. "The Khanty love flat surfaces and the freedom to fantasize."

Claude Clayton Smith

❧ About the American ❧ Editor / Translator

Claude Clayton Smith, Professor Emeritus of English at Ohio Northern University, is the author of eight books and co-editor/translator of two others. His own work has been translated into five languages, including Russian and Chinese. With his late colleague Alexander Vashchenko of Moscow State University, Dr. Smith co-edited *MEDITATIONS After the Bear Feast* (Shanti Arts, 2016) and *The Way of Kinship* (Minnesota, 2010), the world's first anthology of Native Siberian literature. The latter included fiction and nonfiction by Yeremei Aipin, whom they had earlier introduced in the chapbook *I Listen to the Earth* (Ohio Northern University, 1996). In all of these publications, Dr. Smith's role was to polish for an American audience the Russian-to-English translations of Dr. Vashchenko. In the case of the present work, the Russian-to-English translator was Marina Aipina, Yeremei Aipin's daughter.

— claudeclaytonsmith.wordpress.com

SHANTI ARTS

NATURE • ART • SPIRIT

Please visit us online
to browse our entire book
catalog, including poetry
collections and fiction, books
on travel, nature, healing, art,
photography, and more.

Also take a look at our highly
regarded art and literary journal,
Still Point Arts Quarterly, which
may be downloaded for free.

www.shantiarts.com